SHOGOLOGO BABIES

I, _____,
(Your Name)

have read this book

☐ once

☐ twice

☐ again and again

SHOGOLOGO BABIES

A WISE-RIDE Book

by **FLORA A. TREBI-OLLENNU**

pictures by JAN VANDENBERG

Amerley Treb Books

Acknowledgments

To Kwaku Deheer – for great moral support, editing and for listening daily

To Trebi Kuma Ollennu – for research on day names from Ghana and Ivory Coast

To Ashitei Trebi-Ollennu – never tired of editing

To Vashti Achus-Got – for providing day names of the Hausas of Nigeria and Niger

To Ekua Holdbrook Smith & John Yeboah – verification of Fante day names

To Vilma Laryea – verfication of Ewe day names

To Barbara Wibbelmann – editor

ISBN 1-894718-03-8

First Amerley Treb Books printing, January 2002

Printed and bound in Canada by Webcom

To My Twin Children

Trebi Essilfie and Essilfua Deheer

(A Double Blessing)

Auntie Minsher woke

up one morning.

She said,

"I have a painful feeling.

I think, I am going to

have a baby by dusk.

8

That will be Saturday—no,

I crave a Sunday-born."

And, true to her desire, a baby boy,

by Sunday at dawn.

"What shall I name this bundle of delight?

His face radiates with sunlight.

His eyes are keen but cool.

His body is as soft as wool.

He shall be a gentle breeze.

I will call him Kwashie,

I will call him Kwesie.

And if he were a girl

I would call her Ashia."

Auntie Minsher woke

up one morning.

She was served *eyor*,

hot and steaming.

She chuckled under

her breath with a real task.

"I think, I am going to

have a baby by dusk.

That will be Sunday—no,

I crave a Monday-born."

And, true to her desire, a baby girl,

by Monday at dawn.

"What shall I name

this bundle of heaven?

Her face is sweet

and full of giving.

And filled with looks

that will govern.

Her touch as soft

as clouds gently woven.

She shall be pleasant as the sunset.

I will call her Ajua,

I will call her Ajo.

And if she were a boy,

I would call him Kojo."

Auntie Minsher woke

up one morning.

She was served *eyor*,

hot and steaming,

Ringing her bell now and then,

touting her wares from hut to deck.

"Grrr . . . . . I feel

a hunch in my neck.

I think I am going to

have a baby by dusk.

That will be Monday—no,

I crave a Tuesday-born."

And, true to her desire,

a baby boy, Tuesday at dawn.

"What shall I call

this bundle of hope?

His face is sturdy,

his looks say I will cope.

And yet expressions

of tenderness abound

in his eyes. His arms whirl

with energy divinely endowed.

He shall be a mighty wave.

I will call him Korbla,

I will call him Kobina.

And if he were a girl,

I would call her Araba."

Auntie Minsher woke

up one morning.

She was served *eyor*

hot and steaming,

Ringing her bell now and then,

touting her wares from hut to dock.

Under the biggest baobab tree,

she swung in her hammock.

25

"A bee on my nose!" she screeched,

hands over her face like a mask.

"I think, I am going

to have a baby by dusk.

That will be Tuesday—no,

I crave a Wednesday-born."

And, true to her desire,

a baby girl, Wednesday at dawn.

"What shall I name

this bundle of joy?

Her face is lovely,

looks filled with awe,

a touch of gold

from the earth's core,

a saintly gift

without a flaw.

28

She shall be a luscious tree.

I will call her Ekuba,

I will call her Aku.

And if she were a boy,

I would call him Kwaku."

Auntie Minsher woke

up one morning.

She was served *eyor*,

hot and steaming,

Ringing her bell now and then,

touting her wares from hut to dock.

Under the biggest baobab tree

she swung in her hammock.

"Make me corn meal tossed

over okra with a twist.

My, my, my,

what a drool with a fist!

I think, I am going to

have a baby by dusk.

That will be Wednesday—no,

I crave a Thursday-born."

And, true to her desire,

a baby girl, Thursday at dawn.

"What shall I call

this bundle of pleasure?

Her face is charming,

smiles without measure.

Her voice like an angel's,

a unique treasure.

A voice to

lend at leisure.

She shall be a symphony.

I will call her Aba,

I will call her Soyoo.

And if she were a boy,

I would call him Kwao."

Auntie Minsher woke

up one morning.

She was served *eyor*,

hot and steaming,

Ringing her bell now and then,

touting her wares from hut to dock.

Under the biggest baobab tree

she swung in her hammock.

"Make me corn meal tossed

over okra with a twist!"

Out and about, gathering firewood,

she chanced on a beast.

"Oh heavens! I am out of luck.

I need to bask!

I think, I am going to

have a baby by dusk.

That will be Thursday—no,

I crave a Friday-born."

And, true to her desire,

a baby boy, Friday at dawn.

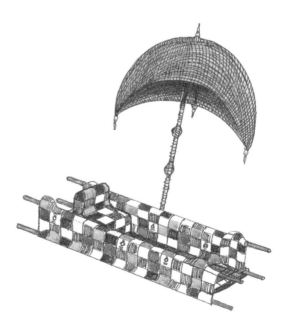

"What shall I name

this bundle of innocence?

His face is laced

with grace in abundance.

His lips move cautiously,

his cheeks dance

with delight. And his arms

are adorned with confidence.

He shall be a noble.

I will call him Kofi,

I will call him Fifi.

And if he were a girl,

I would call her Efiba."

Auntie Minsher woke

up one morning.

She was served *eyor*,

hot and steaming.

44

Ringing her bell now and then,

touting her wares from hut to dock.

Under the biggest baobab tree

she swung in her hammock.

"Make me corn meal tossed

over okra with a twist."

Out and about, gathering firewood,

she chanced on a beast.

"Make me soup churning with

that beast for tonight's feast!"

Suddenly, the beast began to squirm

and squeak over her wrist.

With eyes bulging out she wrest

the beast with a real task.

"I think I am going to

have a baby by dusk.

That will be Friday—no,

I crave a Saturday-born."

And, true to her desire,

a baby girl, Saturday at dawn.

"What shall I call

this bundle of times?

Her face is pure elegance,

hidden behind smiles.

And grace flows over

even into her palms.

Her voice rings

like bell chimes.

She shall be a refreshing brook.

I will call her Amba,

I will call her Ama.

And if she were a boy,

I would call him Kwamena."

Auntie Minsher woke

up one morning.

She did not have

a painful feeling.

She did not chuckle under her

breath with a real task,

she was not out of luck,

she did not need to bask,

she did not screech nor

use her hands as a mask.

Grrrr... she did not

have a hunch in her neck,

There was no drool

with a fist,

she did not have

to wrest a beast.

"Shogologo! Shogologo! Sho...go...lo...go!

I think, I am done having babies."

Auntie Minsher woke

up one morning.

She was served *eyor*,

hot and steaming.

Ringing her bell now and then,

touting her wares from hut to dock.

Under the biggest baobab tree

she swung in her hammock.

"Make me corn meal tossed

over okra with a twist."

Out and about, gathering firewood,

she chanced on a beast.

"Make me soup churning with that

beast for tonight's feast."

With a giggle she licked

her bowl clean with her fist.

"Alas," she said, "I am back to routine."

DID YOU SEE

A palanquin

Gold Crown

Mud stove

Baby

King's staff

Akasha

Horn

Gold coins

Canoe

Royal Arm bracelet

THINK ABOUT IT

What day were you born?

What do you like about the baby born on the same day as you from the story?

Add more descriptions to the baby born on the same day as you?

What do you like about each of the seven babies?

Do you know of a baby not born on any of the seven days of the week?

FLIP OVER, PEEK AND ANSWER

What does Auntie Minsher have for breakfast, lunch and supper?

What work does she do?

What does she do in her spare time?

FIX ME UP SENTENCES

The sentences below are from the story. They'll like to be fixed up just like they read in the story.

1. As wool soft is body his

2. Keen but eyes his cool are

3. Shall gentle be breeze he a

4. Hunch feel in a neck my I Grr…

5. Tuesday crave born a I

6. Nose on bee a my!

7. Drool my fist with my a my what a

8. Symphony shall she be a

9. Hammock swung she in her

10. Shall brook a be refreshing she

RHYME TIME

The word dusk rhymes with the word task. Match the words in the row on the left that rhyme with words on the right. Remember there could be more than one rhyming word.

born	bask
morning	flaw
sunlight	woven
cool	endowed
heaven	feast
neck	treasure
hope	dawn
abound	dusk
dock	task
tree	feeling
mask	deck
twist	wrist
pleasure	cope
abundance	steaming
innocence	hammock
chimes	times
core	bee
	smiles
	wool
	delight
	dance
	measure
	confidence

More Day Names

Hausa (Niger, Nigeria)

	Boy	Girl
Sunday	Dan Ladi	Ladi
Monday	Dan Alti	Altini
Tuesday	Dan Tala	Talatu
Wednesday	Dan Larai	Laraba/Larai
Thursday	Dan Lami	Lami
Friday	Dan Jummai	Jummai
Saturday	Dan Asabe	Asabe

Ewe (Ghana, Togo and Benin)

	Boy	Girl
Sunday	Kosi	Kosiwor
Monday	Kodzo/ Kojo	Ajo/ Adzowo
Tuesday	Kobla / Komla	Abla/ Ablewa
Wednesday	Koku	Aku / Akuwa
Thursday	Yawo/Yao	Yawa/Yawor/Yawo
Friday	Kofi	Afi / Afiwor
Saturday	Komi	Ama

Akan Twi (Ghana, Cote D'Ivoire)

	Boy	Girl
Sunday	Kwesi/Akwesi	Akosua
Monday	Kwadwo	Adwoa
Tuesday	Kwabena	Abena
Wednesday	Kwaku	Akua
Thursday	Yaw	Yaa
Friday	Kofi	Afia
Saturday	Kwame	Ama

Akan Fante (Ghana)

	Boy	Girl
Sunday	Sisi	Esi
Monday	Jojo	Ajoa
Tuesday	Ebo	Araba/Abe
Wednesday	Kuku/Abeku	Kukua
Thursday	Ekow	Aba
Friday	Fifi	Efua/Efe
Saturday	Kwamena/Ato	Amba

Nzema (Ghana, Cote D'Ivoire)

	Boy	Girl
Sunday	Kwesi	Ekessi
Monday	Kojo	Ajoba
Tuesday	Kabela	Abelema
Wednesday	Kaku	Ekuba
Thursday	Kwao	Yaaba
Friday	Kofi	Efiba
Saturday	Kwame	Ama

Ga (Ghana)

	Boy	Girl
Sunday	Kwashie	Ashia
Monday	Kojo	Ajua
Tuesday	Koblah	Abla
Wednesday	Kwaku	Akua
Thursday	Kwao	Aba/Soyoo
Friday	Kofi	Afia
Saturday	Kwame	Ama